Save YOUR *Soul*

ROCHELLE PAIGE

Diane,

Love will
save your
soul!

♡ Rochelle
Paige

Diana,
Love will
Save you
Soul!
♡ Rachel
Page

COPYRIGHT

DEDICATION

To my readers who asked me to write a story for Brecken. Thank you for putting the idea in my head!

Prologue

Hadley

The day I'd discovered my dad was an illegal arms dealer was the worst in my life. Or so I'd thought, until six months later when I woke up to find myself on a cement floor with my arms tied behind my back. When I'd fallen asleep, I'd been safe and sound in my dorm room. I never thought I'd see the day when I regretted my decision to move into a single room instead of a double. If I'd still been in a double, my roommate would have been with me. Or if I'd somehow found a way to forgive my dad, I might have been home with him and my mom, sheltered behind the security of their estate.

After my time in this hellhole, I wasn't sure if I hated my dad more than I had before I'd been kidnapped or less. I'd been beaten the first day, all so they could take pictures to send to him. I didn't understand much of the Spanish they spoke, damn my decision to take French in high school, but their leader took great delight in informing me of the reason I'd been taken in the first place. My father had snubbed him, rejecting a lucrative deal, and I was to be the leverage they used to make him change his mind.

They hadn't really touched me since then, except to force drugs on me a couple times when they needed me to be docile for another photo. The drugs made me easier to control, and I hated how weak I felt afterwards. I couldn't even be certain how many days had passed since I'd been taken. I thought it was thirteen days, but when they gave me the drugs it messed with my head. I might have missed a day or two. Either way, too much time had passed.

There was only one thing I knew for certain. I had no hope of being rescued. Not anymore. I'd been so certain my father would cave to their demands and give them the guns they wanted to save me. Even though I'd screamed hateful words at him the last time we'd spoken, I knew he loved me. He was my father. He would do whatever it took to get me back. *Right?*

Apparently not, because the days had passed without any sign from my captors that he'd yielded to their demands. Their treatment of me hadn't improved in preparation to return me to my family, either. If anything, it had worsened. My meals, if you could call them that, were spaced further and further apart. It felt as though I'd become an afterthought, forgotten by my captors—and my family.

It was all I could to do to survive one day at a time. I was weak and virtually starving. My chances of getting out of this hellhole were slim to none, but I did my best to stay alert. If ever I found an opening, no matter how slight, I was going to take it. I might have been down, but I wasn't out. Not yet. I still had some fight left in me. If nobody was coming for me, then I just needed to figure a way out by myself.

CHAPTER 1

BRECKEN

Two days later...

The Nicaraguan jungle wasn't a place I'd ever hoped to visit. It was hot as hell, unfamiliar territory and buggy as shit. I felt the sweat dripping down my back as quickly as I was wiping it from my forehead. When I'd gotten the call from General Whitehall, asking me to meet with Raymond Gresham about the kidnapping of his daughter, I hadn't wanted to say yes. The team and I had just returned home from a difficult case where we'd been too late to save our target. The oil executive had been killed one day prior to our rescue attempt, and I was pissed the fuck off at the needlessness of his death. If his employer had called us in as soon as they received the ransom demand, we would have arrived in time to save his life. Unfortunately, I didn't deal in *if onlys* in my line of business. Just like I couldn't afford to tell an Army General no when he personally asked me to accept a case, no matter how many questions I had about why he was reaching out to me for help.

When I'd glanced at the photo my client had shown me of his daughter, my hesitation ceased to exist. Only one thing mattered—saving Hadley from the men who'd taken her. The sight of her broad smile and bright green eyes staring up at me from her picture froze me in my tracks. Brown hair so dark it almost appeared black, flowed over her shoulders, stopping just above her tits. Her perky, luscious tits which looked huge on her tiny frame. I got a hard-on from seeing her picture while sitting across from her father and discussing her kidnapping. It was insane. I'd never had a reaction like this to a woman, let alone from a damn picture at a time like this.

It was almost as insane as the feeling of possessiveness which swamped me when Whit whistled softly under his breath while glancing at her picture. We'd been together since boot camp, and I'd been lucky when he decided not to re-up at the same time as me. It meant I was able to open my security firm with Whit at my side, just like I'd started my military career. At his sign of male appreciation, I wanted nothing more than to demonstrate exactly what I'd do if he ever laid a hand on her.

"Back the fuck off," I hissed at him, sending his eyebrows into his hairline before he moved to the wall and leaned against it. I was sure to hear about this later, but I didn't give a fuck. She was mine, but first I needed to get her out of this mess. It had taken me two days to track down her captors and determine where they were most likely holding her. Whit had only mentioned Hadley's looks once, and that was to warn Devon about my reaction to her photo. I was acting out of character, but none of my team called me out on it. They followed my orders and trusted I wouldn't let my fascination with Hadley pull us into a situation we couldn't handle.

Glancing down at my GPS, I confirmed I was less than half a mile from the camp where my intel said she was being held. I'd walked several miles through the jungle since I'd parted from my team, dodging trees and obstacles in my path at a brisk pace. Our recon had indicated that an approach by a lone operator had the best odds of success. In and out with the girl, undetected, that was the plan. With their perimeter security, adding another body upped the chances of exposure. Sera had followed the same route as I'd taken but waited a mile outside the camp. I wanted her close in case Hadley needed the comfort of another woman. It was the smart play, but the need for it made me want to rush into the camp and kill every motherfucker in there.

Devon stayed in town, guarding our transport, while Whit had set up a makeshift clinic. A red haze had clouded my vision at the thought of Hadley needing medical attention, but I'd forced it out of my head and focused on what needed to be done. I couldn't afford to focus on what might have happened to the sexy but sweet girl from the photo, not when her life depended on me keeping a level head. Getting her out of there was going to be tricky enough, but the walk back with Hadley was likely to be worse. She'd been taken in the middle of the night more than two weeks ago. My fists clenched at the thought of what her condition might be when I found her, knowing damn well it wasn't likely to be good. At least I carried appropriate clothing and boots for her in my pack, based on the sizes her mother had provided. If that wasn't good enough, the bottom line was I'd carry her the whole way if that's what it took to get her out of here.

As I neared the target, I slowed my pace and searched for a place to wait until I found the perfect opening. Kneeling down, I lowered myself to my belly in the underbrush. The darkness of the jungle hid my location as I bided my time. Hadley was depending on me, even though she didn't know it, and I wasn't about to let her down. I'd gained a reputation for following through on my missions, and my determination to succeed this time was at an all-time high. I might not have officially met the girl yet, but I was already thinking of her as mine—to rescue, to protect and to keep.

I ran through the plan in my head, weighing all the factors before moving on to plan B, and then C and even D. I was known for being precise in my planning and setting up solid backup plans, but even my team had been surprised by how anal I'd been while preparing for this one. I'd tried to prepare for anything, but I'd experienced enough missions going sideways during my years in the Army to know there was no such thing as a foolproof plan. If this mission went FUBAR,

I needed to know I had enough available options to keep Hadley safe.

I waited until it was a little past midnight and pitch black outside. The camp was silent, with the exception of several guards whose rotation I'd memorized a couple hours ago. The building where Hadley was most likely being kept was the center of the guards' pattern. Nobody had come or gone during the time I'd been watching. I took this as a good sign because it most likely meant that she was alone in there. As soon as the tallest guard rounded the far corner after passing it, I moved swiftly and silently towards the side closest to me. Pulling my E-tool from my pack, I carefully removed two bottom boards, giving me just enough room to squeeze through the opening.

I entered quietly, unsure of what I was going to find in the room, and pulled the boards back into place behind me. Hugging the wall, I held still for a moment and searched the dark room for any sign of Hadley. Going clockwise from the left, my heart was practically in my throat by the time I got to my two o'clock and found a mattress on the floor with a petite body huddled under a thin blanket. She was turned away from me, but I'd recognize that dark hair anywhere. *Thank fuck!* Our intel had been right and I'd found her.

"Hadley," I whispered, dropping to my knees at her side and giving her shoulder a brief touch.

She jerked, rolling away and gasping when her head turned and she caught sight of me. I put my hand over her mouth, silencing her scream. "My name is Brecken Kane. Your father sent me." Her eyes widened, tears leaking from the corners as hope warred with doubt in her gaze. I offered her the only reassurance I could and hoped like hell she'd understand what her father had told me to say. It was for damn sure the silliest code word I've ever used on a mission, but he'd been insistent it was the only thing which would convince her he'd sent me to get her out of here. "Fluffy."

CHAPTER 2

HADLEY

At first I thought I was hallucinating, that I'd finally broken and was seeing things. Then the word the man had spoken penetrated and it dawned on me what was happening. The man, dressed in all black and wearing a large pack on his back, was really here to rescue me. My dad hadn't left me here to die. He'd sent someone to take me home. He could have only been sent by my father because nobody but my parents knew about the puppy I'd owned for one week when I was five years old before we realized I was allergic to her. I'd named her Fluffy and had refused to even so much as consider another name, much to my dad's dismay.

"Thank God," I breathed, the sound muffled by his hand.

The man, Brecken he'd called himself, moved his hand away when the tension left my body. He slid the bag from his back and pulled out a long-sleeved shirt, cargo pants, socks and boots. All black, a perfect match for what he was wearing but much smaller considering his muscular build.

"Take off your night shirt and put these on." His voice was somehow both gentle and abrupt.

"I can't," I admitted softly, moving my wrist and making the chain attached to it clang, drawing his attention to it.

"Fuck," he hissed, eyes sliding to the door my captors used when they needed to come into the room. He was clearly furious on my behalf, and it alleviated some of my embarrassment at my current condition. I was filthy and stinky, dressed in the same oversized nightshirt with a cartoon character on the front and panties I'd worn to bed the night I was taken, and I was chained to a wall in God only knows where. He pulled a tool of some kind from a pocket of his cargo pants and got to work on the lock. Even though I looked and smelled awful, I could have sworn Brecken's eyes flared with desire as he worked to free my hand from the band wrapped around my wrist.

When he was done, he turned his back and gave me privacy to dress. The moment I sat back down after pulling the pants and shirt on, he swiveled towards me and helped me with the socks and boots. We were in the least romantic setting ever, but my heart raced as he kneeled before me. My fingers itched to smooth back a lock of dark hair which had fallen onto his forehead, but I resisted the temptation. It was neither the time nor the place, and I didn't know anything about this man except for his name and that my father trusted him enough to send him after me. Once I was laced up, he touched a button on the watch at his wrist and the face lit up with a countdown showing two minutes remaining.

"Ready to go?"

"Yes." I swallowed down my fear and tried my best to reply in a clear tone, but my voice still wavered. I wasn't sure I would make it far since I hadn't eaten for at least three days, but I was beyond ready to leave this hell hole. He searched my eyes, and I steeled myself to show none of my doubts. I didn't want to give him any reason to leave me behind.

He must have seen what he needed because he nodded his head and led me to the wall next to the bed.

"Wait here."

Here? I looked around the room, confused about how we were going to leave until he dropped to his stomach and slowly eased two boards off the wall. I sunk down to my knees, already tired from the small amount of energy it took to dress and stand. I rested my head on my knees until Brecken reached his hand back through the hole and helped me slink out. Once I was out, he propped the boards against the building and checked the counter on his watch again.

"We need to hurry, precious."

I'd usually argue about a guy using a nickname like precious on me, but it wasn't exactly the right time to say anything. Besides which, I wasn't sure I really wanted to because hearing his rough whisper drop a notch on the word sent butterflies off in my stomach. There hadn't been any chance of me developing Stockholm syndrome over my captors, but it seemed hero worship for Brecken was a definite possibility.

With my hand clutching the back of his shirt, I followed him into the jungle. Brecken radiated so much warmth, I felt it through the material. Even with the long pants and sleeves of the shirt he'd given me and the unrelenting heat outside, I was chilled. It seemed like forever ago since I'd felt warm. I stifled a laugh at the image of me using Brecken as a blanket.

The one my captors had given me hadn't been much help, but I was pretty sure the feel of his arms around me would heat me up in no time flat.

Biting my chapped bottom lip, I scolded myself for my thoughts as I followed behind him. If he had a plan to get me out of here, I wasn't going to do anything to slow him down—and that included paying attention to where we were going instead of ogling his ass. In an effort to limit the temptation he presented, I moved my hand from his shirt and placed it on his backpack instead.

We moved quickly, reaching the protection the jungle provided without detection. I breathed a sigh of relief and then gasped for air when Brecken stopped dead in his tracks and held up one hand. When he placed a finger towards the bottom of his ear and cocked his head, I realized he was in contact with someone else and hadn't come alone. I glanced over my shoulder, terrified that one of the guards would notice I was missing before we'd gotten far enough away.

"Fuck!" Brecken hissed, drawing my attention back to him and freaking me the fuck out.

"What?" I whispered when he dropped his hand to his side, my heart pounding so hard it felt like it was about to jump out of my chest.

"A member of my team is a mile out in the same direction I'd planned to take you," he replied, pulling me in front of him and turning me to the left. "She spotted a convoy headed this way."

He nudged me forward until we were standing next to a large tree. "What kind of convoy?"

"She couldn't get close enough to tell without running the risk of giving her position away. All I know is that three vehicles are heading in as fast as they can on the shitty ass road,"—he stopped to point over his shoulder—"about a quarter of a mile that way. The road dumps straight into the compound, so this has to be their destination. And we can't afford to be here when they arrive."

The answer seemed obvious to me. "Then let's go meet up with your friend and get the heck out of here."

"We can't." His tone brooked no room for argument, not like I was going to disagree anyway. He was the expert here. "It would take us too long to reach her, and that's the direction they're most likely to assume we've gone since the closest town is that way. She's already on her way to warn the other two men I brought with me, and we're moving to plan D."

"Plan D?" *What happened to B and C?*

"We're going to circle part-way around the camp and head into the deepest part of the jungle."

I swatted yet another bug away from my neck and cringed at the idea of spending even more time in this God forsaken jungle. "Okay." My voice shook with fear, and Brecken reacted by bending down to stare straight into my eyes while reaching for my hand and giving it a squeeze.

"As long as we're careful to limit the tracks we leave behind, this is the last route they'll expect us to take because it's the hardest and longest one."

Hard and long. My gaze dropped to his crotch and then I lowered it to the ground like that was what I'd intended all along. Geesh! What was it about this guy that was making my hormones go crazy? He was talking about marching me through the jungle in my weakened state for who knew how long, and I'd actually taken the time to check out his package. It was official—either I was an idiot or I really did have a white knight complex.

"Stay right here." He squeezed my hand one more time before letting go and pulling my nightshirt from his pack. "I'm going to lay a false trail but it will only take a few minutes."

Watching him walk away was one of the hardest things I'd ever done. I wanted to beg him to take me with him, to let me help. The only thing holding me back was the knowledge that I wouldn't be any help to him at all, only a hindrance. Freezing my muscles in place, I closed my eyes and thought about the periodic table of elements. It was something I'd taken to doing since I'd been taken. For some odd reason, reciting it in my mind helped to calm me down each time I'd started to freak out. It wasn't until I'd reached Iodine that I felt his hand on my elbow and opened my eyes again.

"Ready?"

I nodded swiftly.

"I won't lie to you, the next couple days are going to be tough as hell, but I'm going to get you through this and back home safe and sound."

Safe and sound was an excellent concept, but I didn't think a place like that existed for me anymore. I wasn't sure how much he knew about my dad's business, so I kept my mouth shut and offered him a weak smile instead.

He turned away from me and placed my hand on his lower back, his body heat warming my hand once again. "Stay right behind me."

"You're not about to lose me. I'll follow you anywhere you take me."

Chapter 3

Brecken

Blood pumped through my veins at her vow. My brain knew it was motivated by my rescue of her, but my cock didn't give a damn why she'd said it. He wanted her to follow him straight to the nearest flat surface. I glanced at the ground and shook my head. Or vertical would work. A tree was something I could work with if I leaned back on it so the bark couldn't damage her skin. I caught myself considering a tree about twenty feet ahead of us when I realized what I was doing.

Down boy! I needed to get my head out of her panties and back on the mission before she paid the price for my distraction. Once she was safe, I could think about making her mine. After I made sure she was comfortable—checked over every delectable inch of her body to make sure she hadn't sustained any serious injuries, got some much-needed water into her and gave her as much food as she could handle. She was still a fucking knockout, but she'd lost enough weight since she'd been taken that it was clearly visible. Her cheekbones were more pronounced and her tits weren't nearly as full as they'd been in the photo her dad had given me. The same picture I carried with me because I couldn't bear to let go of it.

Shoving the raging desire I felt for Hadley down, I trekked forward. There was no sign they'd detected her disappearance from the camp yet, but I couldn't bank on our luck holding much longer. We needed to put as much distance between us and them as possible. I felt like shit for doing it, but I set a grueling pace which I knew would be hard for Hadley even if she'd been one hundred percent. I heard her breathing quicken behind me, but she didn't offer a word in protest and kept her hand wrapped tightly in my shirt.

We made it about a mile before I heard her muttering underneath her breath, reciting the periodic table. The check I'd done on her had revealed she was a chemistry major, biochemistry to be more specific. A little bit of extra digging had uncovered her intention to make her career in cancer research. If my reaction to her photo had been strange, the pride I felt about her life goals was even odder. Respect for her desire to help others would have made sense, but what I'd felt was deeper than that. It was similar to the reaction I was having to how she was handling our march through the jungle. My precious girl was one hell of a woman.

Another half mile later, Hadley stumbled. I stopped and turned to make sure she was okay. She managed to stay upright, but I could tell she wasn't going to be able to make it much further. When she waved me on, letting me know she was fine, I marched forward once again but at a slower pace. I kept an eye out for a good place to rest and heaved a deep sigh of relief when I spotted a fallen tree trunk on the ground fifteen minutes later.

"We need to take a break," I explained, leading her to the spot and helping her sit down.

"I know I do," she sighed. "But I'm pretty sure you're part robot and could keep walking forever."

Her eyes were lit with humor and held a hint of female appreciation as she looked up at me. Her skin was shiny with sweat, her face bright red from the heat and exertion, bug bites were visible on her hands and neck and yet she sat there cracking jokes. My heart swelled with that unfamiliar feeling once again. *Had there ever been a more perfect woman to walk this Earth than Hadley?* It was hard for me to imagine there was.

I dropped my pack to the ground and dug through it for supplies. "There were many occasions when I was in the Army when being part robot would have been a big help."

"You were in the Army?" She laughed lightly, looking surprised by my response.

"Yeah." I kept my answer simple, not wanting to get into what I did during my time there. The training I'd received and the missions I'd gone on provided me with invaluable experience that I was putting to good use with my company, but I didn't want the things I saw and did back then to touch Hadley in any way.

She took the canteen I held out with a shaky hand, drinking from it greedily. "Slow down," I murmured, wrapping my fingers around the hand holding the canteen and moving it away from her plump lips. "If you drink too quickly, you'll get sick."

"Crap, sorry," she muttered. "I know better, but it's been too long since I've tasted anything so good. I promise I'll slow down."

Her free hand came up to gently pry my fingers away, and I wanted to complain at the lost contact. Her skin was chilled, and I wanted to strip her out of the clothes I'd brought her and warm her up the best way I knew how—with as much direct skin-to-skin contact as possible. With her naked body writhing against mine. When I handed her a protein bar from my pack, the look on her face made me feel like a monster for letting my little head do the thinking and delaying, even for a minute, getting some food into her stomach when she was starving. Literally starving, judging from the way her eyes lit as though I'd conjured up a lobster tail, which I knew was her favorite meal since I'd left no stone unturned when it came to finding out as much about her as I could. The protein bars I'd brought weren't the best tasting, but her little moans as she slowly ate it told me how much she appreciated the meal, such as it was.

"I should have brought some MREs with me." Hadley cocked her head and raised an eyebrow questioningly, still chewing on the last bite she'd taken. Perched on a tree trunk in the middle of the jungle, she still managed to have the manners of a princess. With each passing minute, I was more determined to get her out of this jungle and back home where I could treat her like one.

"Meals ready to eat," I explained. "Not that they taste any better than the protein bars, they're worse actually, but at least they'd give you the illusion of eating a meal."

She swallowed the last bite and beamed up at me, patting her stomach. "As wonderful as you've made an MRE sound, I don't think I could handle one since I'm completely full."

She was so damn sweet, and it killed me to know the only reason she was full from a fucking protein bar was because they hadn't fed her enough. Her stomach had to have shrunk a ton over the last two weeks. I didn't know what else they'd put her through, but I was going to find out soon. First, I needed to know if she could handle a couple more miles. The sun was rising already, light shining through the trees above us and we needed to make more progress before the killer afternoon heat in a few hours.

Sinking to my knees in front of her, I slowly reached one hand out to her knee.

She flinched, a reflexive action I tried not to take personally, and then held still. "How are the boots working for you? Not too small? No blisters?"

She jerked her head back and forth but kept her eyes locked on me.

"Do you think you can handle a few more miles?"

She gave me a quick nod in the affirmative, fear and shame still alive in her eyes. I gritted my teeth, holding back the howl of rage which crept up my throat. If I'd brought my sniper rifle with me on this mission, there would be no doubt the guys who'd taken her would have gotten what was coming to them after we'd made it to safety. I tried my best to not let my anger show outwardly, the last thing I wanted to do was scare Hadley any more than she already was. I wanted to be her rock. The person she turned to for comfort. The one who made her feel safe. And the man who kept her out of harm's way. If that meant waiting to kill those motherfuckers, then so be it. But one day Hadley's vengeance would be mine.

CHAPTER 4

HADLEY

The look on Brecken's face was fierce, and for some reason I took comfort in it. Deep down inside, I knew his anger wasn't directed at me. No, it was on my behalf. I felt horribly guilty for flinching away from his touch. He'd rescued, clothed and fed me. At no point had he done anything to harm me. I knew this, and yet I couldn't stop myself from tensing up the second I realized he was going to touch me. But once I felt the warmth of his hand on my leg, I wanted more. The contradictory feelings were enough to make my head spin—my heart and mind at war with each other. Swallowing down my fear, my voice croaked a bit when I spoke.

"I can make it as far as you need me to go."

I was surprised to find it was true. I was beyond exhausted and ached all over, but with Brecken by my side and some food and water in me much of my self-doubt had disappeared. I'd survived my kidnapping. Brecken had rescued me. The least I could do for him was find whatever strength I needed to make our escape go as smoothly as possible. I could do this. No, I *would* do this, come hell or high-water as my mom always said.

"You sure? Because I can carry you if need be."

I shivered at the thought of Brecken having a better reason to carry me, other than our tromp through the jungle—like on our way to a bed. If we'd met any other way, I didn't think he'd look at me twice. In the light of the morning, I'd gotten a much better look at Brecken and couldn't help but believe he was way out of my league. Tall, dark, ruggedly handsome, muscular and confident. Really, the list of his attributes could go on and on. And on some more.

I was cute, in a nerdy kind of way. I was a late bloomer and still saw myself as I'd been in high school, flat chested with braces and no sense of my personal style. Enough guys had asked me out once I was in college and away from home for me to know I was attractive, but I hadn't fared well in the dating scene. Socially awkward didn't go far enough to explain my personality. Put me anywhere near a hot guy, and you'd be guaranteed to find me blushing and stammering. Maybe even tripping over the ground or pouring something all over myself. Or on the nearby hottie, which had happened more times than I liked to admit.

Who knew my kidnapping would rid me of my awkwardness? At least around Brecken. He'd already seen me at my worst, literally. It was oddly freeing to know there wasn't anything else I could do to make me look worse in his eyes. The very same ones which flashed with heat and approval when he looked at me. I refused to let him down and lose the fluttering in my belly when he glanced at me.

"I'm positive. Lead on, Macduff."

He helped me to my feet, chuckling deeply. "Hopefully we won't need to fight to the death. But if we do, you can be damn sure I'll stand between you and anything which intends you harm."

Holy crap! He'd gotten my nerdy Macbeth reference. With that, he'd managed to be even hotter. Add in his determination to keep me safe, and those butterflies took flight again right along with my heart which melted. Brecken didn't realize the impact of his words on me. He went about the business of getting us out of here, leading the way through the jungle once again, while the foundation of my world seemed to shift with him at the center.

I trudged behind him for the seemingly endless march. We'd walked for what felt like forever, until the sun was high in the sky and my clothes were drenched with sweat. I heard the sound of running water in the distance, making my mouth water with thirst. Brecken held up a hand, signaling me to stop, and pulled a set of binoculars out of a pants pocket. He scanned the distance ahead of us before swiveling in a full circle to search the jungle. The foliage was so thick, I wasn't sure if he could even see anything in some locations, but he took his time and did a thorough check before dropping the binoculars back in his pocket.

"There's a waterfall ahead."

Except for the moment when I'd heard him say "Fluffy" and realized he was there to rescue me, I'd never heard sweeter words. A waterfall meant water. Hopefully clean water I could drink. And if lady luck was on my side, maybe even use to clean off a little bit. I hadn't bathed for more than two weeks, and I'd practically kill to get clean. My hope must have shone from my eyes because Brecken grinned at me.

"Yeah, I thought you'd like the sound of that."

Heck yes, I did!

"We need to stop and rest soon anyway."

I liked the sound of that even better.

"It's getting too hot for us to keep going without running the risk of overheating and dehydrating. There hasn't been any sign of us being followed. If we're lucky, there will be a cave behind the waterfall where we can rest for the day, wait out the hottest hours of the day before we go further."

I felt like sobbing with gratitude. Brecken wasn't showing any signs of needing to slow down. He was as sure-footed as he'd been when we first started out. While I gasped for breath, he didn't seem winded at all. If we were stopping to rest, it was because he was concerned for me. A part of me wanted to tell him I didn't need to stop, that we could keep going, but I couldn't bring myself to say the words. I was too busy nodding my agreement and trying not to cry. If I could even manage tears, I wasn't sure I was hydrated enough for my body to manufacture any.

When we reached the waterfall, I almost fell to my knees in gratitude. It spilled into a small lake, filled with crystal clear water. "Please tell me we can drink it."

Brecken pulled a couple white tablets out of a pocket. He seemed to have everything in those darn things. He dropped them into his canteen and filled it with water. "In thirty minutes it will be." Then he pulled another tablet out of a different pocket and dropped it into the water. "And this will help with the iodine flavor so we'll be able to choke it down more easily."

A nervous giggle crept up my throat as I thought about something else I'd like to choke down. It was even something he was packing in his pants, just not in one of the endless pockets he seemed to have. My laughter earned me a strange look from Brecken, and I was glad he couldn't read my mind. How embarrassing would it be for him to discover the clueless virgin he'd rescued was picturing herself on her knees in front of him with his cock shoved down her throat? Talk about taking awkward to a whole new level. Or maybe not, considering I was almost sure I'd spotted a half-chub in those pants a time or two when I'd glanced his way.

Taking a deep breath and getting a good whiff of myself, I wasn't sure how it was possible for him to be attracted to me like this. I glanced at the pool of water longingly and Brecken caught my look.

"Go ahead and get cleaned up, but make sure to keep your clothes dry. You'll need to get dressed as soon as you're out, and I don't have a spare set for you to use. I don't want us to be caught at a major disadvantage out in the open like this."

There was only one way I could think to keep my clothes dry. "Can you turn around please?"

His dark eyes scanned my body, flaring with heat before he swiveled on a heel and gave me his back. I quickly stripped out of my boots and clothes, leaving them on a rock near the edge of the water. Once I'd moved far enough that my body was covered, I called out to Brecken. "The coast is clear."

He was quick to face me again, his eyes locking on me right away. "So is the water."

I glanced down, only to find my naked body clearly visible. "Crap!"

"You're fucking adorable, precious."

It was a compliment a guy might give his little sister, but the way he was looking at me was anything but brotherly. It put thoughts into my head, naughty thoughts I'd never had for any of the guys I'd gone on dates with in the past. It's probably the other part of why I'd never had any second dates. I'd never felt chemistry like this with anyone before Brecken. After my kidnapping, I was determined to make the most out of each day I had because I wasn't sure how many more I had. For all I knew, today could be my last.

"What are the odds of us making it out of this safe and sound?"

Brecken's gaze jerked up to search my face. He moved closer to the water and bent down so we were closer to eye level with each other. "They're damn good, Hadley. The route we're taking is one I'd planned on using if it became necessary. We aren't flying blind here. My team will be waiting for us, ready to get us the hell out of here as soon as we reach them."

"What if the bad guys catch up to us first?"

"Then they'll have to go through me to get to you, and I'm not an easy man to kill."

He wasn't saying they wouldn't find us. When I'd been taken, one of the things I regretted the most was my virginity. I lived in fear of it being taken from me by force. There wasn't anything I could do about it then, but here with Brecken was a different story. One in which I was determined to take control—at least for as long as Brecken would give it to me.

CHAPTER 5

BRECKEN

When Hadley had gotten into the water, she'd been so damn shy, sweetly asking me to turn around so I wouldn't see her nudity. Something changed in the short time while she washed, though. As she strode out of the lake, buck ass naked with all her luscious curves on display for me, there was a determined look in her eyes as she stared at me. It took all my restraint to hold still after rising to my feet when she passed up her pile of clothes and kept coming towards me. She stopped a few inches away, close enough that I could easily bend down and lick away one of the water drops dripping down her tits. Or all of them, that was a much better plan. Drying her with my lips and hands before she got dressed, maybe taking the time to give her an orgasm or two. I was so wrapped up in my own fantasies of what I wanted to do to Hadley that I almost didn't catch what she said, and missing her request would have been a fucking travesty.

"I want to sleep with you."

Sleep. She'd said sleep. My cock assumed she meant fucking and quickly hardened, but maybe she meant she was tired and felt safer letting her guard down with me than without. Considering what she'd gone through, it would certainly make more sense.

"Let me check out the cave and then you can rest," I croaked out.

The gentle smile she gave me was blinding in its beauty. Her eyes lit with laughter and she shook her head. "No, Brecken. I mean I want to *sleep* with *you.*"

My cock figured it out faster than my brain, pressing so hard against my zipper that I wouldn't be surprised if it left an imprint behind. My precious angel wanted to have sex with me. Now. Her cheeks pinkened, and a hint of uncertainty entered her gaze, making me take that final step which brought her body flush with mine. The timing was piss poor, and I was probably taking advantage of the situation, but I wasn't about to let her think, even for a minute, that I didn't want her.

"Get back in the water, my precious girl." She looked crushed by my answer, and I hurried to explain. "Swim over to the other side of the waterfall. It will provide us with some cover. I'll move your things into the cave and do one final sweep to make sure nobody is going to sneak up on us anytime soon."

Before she could turn away from me, I claimed her mouth with a deep kiss. I'd intended to show her exactly how much I wanted her, but I'd seriously underestimated the strength of my desire because the kiss turned explosive the second my lips touched hers. It quickly spiraled out of control, with my hands sliding down her bare back to her ass and lifting her up until her pussy lined up with my cock. She wrapped her legs around my waist and ground against me while I thrust upwards.

When I tore my mouth from hers, she mewled in protest and the sound of her need had me dropping to my knees in front of her. Her glistening pink pussy was inches from my mouth, wet from the lake and the proof of her desire for me. Running my nose up her folds, a growl rumbled up my throat at the scent of her cream. Gripping her ass in one hand, I parted her with the fingers of my other hand and gave her a slow lick from top to bottom, dipping into her hole with my stiffened tongue. Holding her pussy open for my mouth, I used my tongue and teeth to build Hadley up until she was moaning and her legs were trembling. When I sunk a finger into her, knuckle deep, she screamed my name as she shattered. Licking and sucking, I let her ride my face through her orgasm. Rising to my feet afterwards, my chin was wet with her juices and my cock was iron hard with the need to feel her soft wetness wrapped around me.

"Water, now," I ordered her in a growl. "Be damn careful in there. Don't let me out of your sight until you make it through the waterfall."

I kept an eagle eye on her as she walked back into the lake, gathering up her clothes and marching around the water and climbing over the rocks to get behind the waterfall. I found a small cave, the perfect place for us to rest out of the sun today—after I fucked her incredibly tight pussy. I might be an ass for taking advantage of her vulnerability this way, but Hadley was going to be mine one way or another. It had been a done deal from the moment I saw her picture. The situation had just sped things along a little, shortening the wait until the inevitable.

I helped Hadley out of the water, settling her on my spare shirt so her delicate skin wouldn't chafe on the rough floor. I handed her the canteen and another protein bar. "Don't forget to drink slowly," I reminded her, bending over to bite a nipple, enjoying the sight of the red mark when I lifted my head. "Wait here for me while I do a perimeter check."

Her bottom lip popped out in an adorable pout. "Your safety comes first, precious." I lifted one of her hands and placed her palm on my hard length, making her eyes widen in surprise. "It will be hell to walk around like this, but well worth it to know you're protected."

"Okay," she whispered.

The innocence in her gaze had me moving her hand away and offering her an out I hadn't intended to give. "What happens when I get back is entirely up to you, Hadley. If you decide you aren't ready for more, I'll understand. No matter what, I'll get you to safety."

"What about you?" she asked, lifting her hand to my dick again. "I came but you didn't."

"I count myself fucking lucky for getting to taste you." I lowered my head and growled into her ear, "In fact, if you want it again, I'd happily spend the whole afternoon eating your little pussy."

Her fingers clenched against my shoulders. "What if I want a taste of you?"

My cock hardened more, if that was even possible. "Later," I promised. "I'm definitely going to want your pink lips wrapped around my dick, but not yet."

Her head tilted back. "I thought you said it was up to me what happened next?" she teased.

"That I did," I agreed. "But I want your pussy first. And you want to give me that, don't you Hadley?"

She shivered, nodding in agreement with a dazed look on her face. "Yeah," she sighed.

"As soon as I get back."

"Hurry," she urged, making me move faster.

I forced myself to slow down and take my time as I checked the surrounding area for any signs of danger. I couldn't afford to let my cock force me into making a mistake, not with Hadley depending on me. Each lick of my lips, tasting her on them, reminded me of what was at stake.

It took me longer than I liked, leaving her alone in the cave, but when I headed back, I was convinced we were safe for the time being. I couldn't find any sign we'd been followed, and it was close enough to my predetermined check-in time for me to reach out to my team. I clicked on the communication device in my ear, activating it since it had been turned off to ensure we couldn't be tracked using the signal. Whit must have been waiting for my contact because his voice came on the line right away.

"Which route did you end up taking, Boss?"

"We used Plan D."

"Shit, that one was a bitch of a trek. How's the girl holding up?"

"It's none of your damn business how *my* girl is going," I hissed.

"Whit was just being an ass, Brecken. We all know she's your girl," Sera attempted to soothe me. "But we won't be able to get to you guys for at least another day depending on your progress, so we kinda need to know how's she's doing."

"Better than a lot of soldiers would be under the same circumstances." My pride in Hadley came through loud and clear. "At the pace we've gone so far, we should be at the extraction point by tomorrow afternoon."

"Time's up, Boss." We did our best to keep our communications under a minute to avoid detection.

"We'll be ready and waiting," Sera promised before disconnecting.

"You better be." The words were for my benefit only, a good thing too because they dried up in my throat at the sight which greeted me once I'd made it over the rocks and behind the waterfall. Hadley waited for me, dressed in my spare shirt and her boots. The shirt rode up her legs, and her pussy was visible to me from this angle.

"What did you decide?" I growled out, frozen in place and knowing I'd need to jump into the water to cool off if she said no.

"Yes."

Thank fuck!

CHAPTER 6

HADLEY

It wasn't exactly the sexiest look ever, but I didn't have a lot of options and sitting here naked by myself in the middle of the jungle seemed like the height of stupidity. I didn't want to risk getting caught by someone else without any clothes on, but I also wanted to look hot when Brecken returned. As awkward as I felt sitting here like this, it was well worth it when I saw the look in his eyes when he came back. Even more so when he set his weapons down, unlaced his boots and kicked them off, with his cargo pants, boxers and shirt following shortly after.

"Let me get cleaned up first." I only had a moment to appreciate the view before he jumped in the water. When he came back up for air, my breath stilled in my lungs at how utterly gorgeous he was. Slipping off my boots and moving to the ledge that dropped off into the water, I asked the question I'd been wondering about since we'd met.

"Why do you call me precious?"

"Because that's exactly what you are to me. You have been from the moment your dad handed me a photo of you."

With his words, any lingering traces of doubt were wiped from my heart and mind. I whipped his shirt off my body and jumped into the water, straight into his arms. My naked chest pressed against his until I leaned back and he took advantage of the new position, licking and sucking on my tits. My nipples beaded into hard nubs, and it had nothing to do with the cold water and everything to do with the feel of Brecken's hot mouth on my skin.

I moaned, thrusting my chest forward, my hands clutching his shoulders and gripping tightly. My nails dug into his skin as I writhed in his arms, legs wrapped around his waist.

"Easy, precious," he chuckled. "I'm not going anywhere."

I trembled at the sensual threat in his voice. The whole world felt like it was spinning out of control, but I felt safe here in his arms, in our own private paradise. "Promise?"

"Where would I go when I've got you right where I want you?"

I glanced up at the cave and then back down into Brecken's eyes. "Can we have sex in here, though?"

He lowered me down his chest until my pussy rested over his hardened length. "Yeah, precious. We can definitely have sex in the water. Considering how tight you felt around my finger, it's probably a good idea."

"Good," I sighed. "Because I don't want to wait a second longer."

The muscles in his arms flexed as his arms tightened around me. "I did promise you could decide what happened when I got back."

"Yes, you did," I giggled.

"You've never done it in water before?" I shook my head, my heart racing when I realized he didn't know this was my first time in water or on land. Anywhere. "Then hold on tight."

His finger dipped into my hole, finding me drenched and distracting me from what I knew I needed to tell him. His thumb circled my clit while his mouth lavished my tits with attention. Gripping my hips, he lined his dick up with my pussy until the tip rested at my opening. The sensual fog cleared for a moment, as I realized this was really going to happen.

Right now. Brecken was going to take my virginity and I hadn't even told him.

"This is my first—"

My words turned into a cry when he slammed me down, tearing through the proof of my virginity.

"Hadley, you should have told me," he moaned, trying to jerk backwards at the realization of what just happened. I locked my legs around his waist, refusing to let him leave me. The worst of the pain was lessening already, and I wanted the pleasure I knew he could give me. I wiggled my hips back and forth, trying to find a comfortable position. It might be an impossible task because I felt like his dick was about to split me in two.

"Be still," he ordered, teeth clenched so hard it created white brackets around his mouth. "You need time to adjust to my size."

"You're huge," I breathed out. I'd thought he was big based on the glimpse I'd gotten of him before he'd jumped into the water, but I'd never expected him to feel quite so large once he was inside me. "I swear I can feel you all the way up to my stomach, Brecken."

"You can't say stuff like that right now," he groaned. "I'm trying my best to wait until the pain passes. I'm sorry, precious. If I'd known, I would have been gentler. I never want to do anything that causes you pain."

"It's not like there was another way," I breathed into his ear, jerking my hips slightly and whimpering. "It would have hurt no matter what and I'm glad it's you causing the pain because I wouldn't have wanted it to be anyone else."

His fingers dug into my sides, his eyes filled with a possessive gleam as he stared down at me. "There's nobody else for you, Hadley. Only me. You're mine and you're damn well never going to think about another man seeing you like this." He paused to lean down and suck on a nipple, long and hard until he'd left a mark behind. "I'll kill any man who tries."

My pussy clenched, clearly in favor of being owned by Brecken.

"You like that, don't you?" he breathed against my other nipple, nipping and sucking at it. "Wearing my marks and knowing I'll never let another man touch you."

"Yes," I moaned.

"You're getting wetter around me. Your body knows exactly what it wants." He pulled partially out of me, the slide of his hot, hard skin against my inner walls making me shudder. Then he plunged back in and I cried out, in pleasure this time instead of pain. "My precious girl, taking my cock like you were made for it even though it's your first time."

I never thought I'd be a fan of dirty talk, but hearing Brecken brought me close to the edge. He was thrusting up hard enough to slam me down on his dick with each drive of his hips.

"Please, please, please," I chanted frantically. I was so close to coming, needing something to push me over the edge, but I didn't know what it was. Then his hand slid between us, one finger circling my clit and I screamed his name as my body shuddered in his arms. My pussy clenched down hard on his cock, and I turned my head for a kiss, needing to feel his lips on mine as I flew apart. He continued to pound into me, and I screamed into his mouth as a second wave struck, stronger than anything I'd ever felt before.

"Hadley," Brecken shouted, shoving my knees wider and ramming in deeper a few more times before exploding.

"Mine," he growled into my ear.

My voice was whisper soft when I answered. "Yes, Brecken. I'm yours." It was true, I'd surrendered more than my virginity to him under this water. Somehow, I'd managed to give him my heart too.

CHAPTER 7

BRECKEN

Holy fuck! That was the best goddamn sex I'd ever had. In the middle of the jungle, with a virgin. Not just any virgin, either. This was Hadley. If I hadn't already known it, the way my heart pounded when I realized no other man had been inside her before me would have clinched it. As much as it killed me to know I'd hurt her, I rejoiced in the knowledge that I was going to be the only man to ever have her. Every possessive tendency which had lain dormant inside of me before her had roared to the surface.

Hadley was mine. Period, end of story, and she had my come filling her pussy to prove it. I'd taken her bare, the first time in my life I'd ever gone without a condom. I couldn't bring myself to regret it, either. The feel of her hot, wet pussy wrapped around my cock was better than I'd imagined it would be, and I'd done a lot of fantasizing about her since I'd seen her photo. Too much apparently, since I hadn't been able to resist taking her the way I had.

"Fuck, precious."

"What?" she murmured drowsily against my neck, her head resting on my shoulder.

"You in any pain?"

She wiggled against me before settling back in my arms and sighing. "Nope. I'm feeling pretty amazing, actually."

I moved us towards the ledge and lifted Hadley off me, not missing her wince when my cock slid out of her. I raised her up and set her down on the edge. "Amazing, huh?"

I lifted one of her feet, searching for any sign of blisters. When I didn't find any, I slid my hands up her calves, around her knee and along her inner thigh.

"That tickles," she gasped, jerking her leg out of my grasp.

"I'll have to remember how ticklish you are," I murmured, lifting her other foot and repeating the process again.

"Like you need to use tickling as a weapon against me when you have much more dangerous ones already."

"Like what?" I asked distractedly, shifting my search higher.

"Your eyes, your face, your shoulders, your chest, your ass, your voice," she listed off, surprising me. "Your lips, your tongue, your fingers, and your dick."

She whispered the last word, and I looked up from my examination of her ribs, which were too prominent for my liking, to find her blushing adorably. "You're not without your own weapons, my precious girl."

"I'm not, huh?" She flashed a dimpled grin at me, cocking her head to the side. "What's a girl like me got that will hold up against a man like you?"

Sliding my hands around her back, I stepped closer to her and lifted her knees to my sides. "I probably shouldn't admit this to you, but you've got a whole arsenal you could use against me and I'd be helpless to resist. Something you've already proven,"—I pointed over my shoulder with a thumb—"by seducing me under a waterfall when I should be focused on keeping you safe while you get some much-needed rest."

"I'd rather do what we just did than sleep."

I slid one hand up and swiped a thumb under her eye, right over the dark circle there. "Part of being mine, my precious girl, is letting me do what's best for you. Your well-being comes before anything and everything."

"Even amazing sex?"

"Yeah, even then," I chuckled before getting serious again. "Speaking of which, I wish you'd told me you were a virgin."

"I tried," she protested softly. "Sort of, right at the last minute. But I waited too long and then you were inside me and you already knew."

She was so damn adorable, it was hard to be tough on her. I steeled myself to get my point across because what I needed to say to her was important. "I'm sure you had your reasons for not sleeping with anyone before today, Hadley, and I for one am damn happy you did because I'm the one who benefited from your decision. I can even understand why you were hesitant to tell me about your virginity, Hadley. But no more," my voice firmed. "If it has something to do with your comfort or safety, then you can't hold information back from me. No matter if you find it embarrassing or awkward to talk about."

"You can't just order me to talk to you about everything," she huffed.

"I can." I climbed out of the water, lifting her into my arms and carrying her into the cave. Sitting down, leaning my back against the wall, I settled her on my lap. "In fact, I just did."

"Yeah, yeah, yeah," she grumbled. "You're lucky you're so hot or else I wouldn't let you get away with stuff like this."

"Lucky for me you think I'm hot."

"Oh, please," she laughed. "I don't *think* you're hot, I know it. Just like I know any woman out there would agree with me."

"I don't care what other women think, Hadley." I dropped a kiss on the top of her head. "Just you."

"You're too good to be true," she whispered sleepily, followed by a deep yawn. "I'm afraid to fall asleep and wake up to find out you're not real. To wake up in that bed with the chain on my wrist and discover you're only a dream."

"I'm real, my precious girl." I tightened my arms around her, pissed off at the thought of her being scared to sleep. "And I'm not going anywhere. I'll be right here when you wake up."

She tilted her head to look up at me, her eyes drifting closed. "Promise?"

"You couldn't get rid of me now if you tried," I answered.

"Don't wanna anyway." Her head dropped back onto my chest, her eyes remaining shut while the beat of her heart evened out.

"Not yet, you don't." I waited until I knew she was asleep and wouldn't hear me finish my thought. "But I don't think you've figured out yet that I mean to keep you forever. And when you do, you may change your mind. Not that it will make a difference after you gave yourself to me."

She sighed in her sleep and cuddled deeper into my chest. "Hell, as long as I'm confessing my secrets, it wouldn't have mattered before then either. Your fate was sealed the moment I laid eyes on your photo."

I enjoyed the feel of her in my arms for as long as was safe before pulling her shirt over her head. She barely moved when I tugged her pants up her legs, put her socks and boots on, lacing them up. Then I laid her down on the ground on top of my spare shirt, using my pack as a pillow. She barely stirred through it all. I'd known she was tired but hadn't realized the extent of her exhaustion.

Once I got her settled, I got dressed and did a quick survey of the surrounding area. There was still no sign of trouble, which meant I figured I could afford to give Hadley an extra hour of sleep. I spent that time finishing up the water in my canteen and refilling it before eating a couple protein bars, staring at her the entire time. It was a sight I'd never grow tired of. Not in a million years. Hadley was my salvation, the prize I earned for the shit I had to do in the Army. And nobody was going to take her away from me. Unfortunately, that meant I needed to wake her up and get us back on the trail so we could get the hell out of this jungle.

I gently shook her shoulder, bending down to whisper in her ear. "Sorry, precious, but we gotta go."

Her eyes popped open, and she blinked up at me a couple times before sitting up. The first thing she did was look down and laugh when she noticed she was dressed. "Holy crap, I really must have been zonked out."

I'd said it before, and I'd say it again—she was too fucking adorable. "I told you that you needed the sleep."

"Nobody likes a know-it-all," she complained, getting to her feet and dusting the dirt off her lush ass.

I chuckled at her annoyance, earning myself a dirty look. "Not quite true since you like me."

She tried to hold her glare, but her lip curled up on the sides and her eyes filled with humor. "Didn't you say something about us needing to leave?"

My heart filled with pride again at her acceptance of the situation as I reached out for her hand and she placed it in mine. "Let's go."

We headed back into the jungle, hand-in-hand, with a long way to go before we were safe.

Chapter 8

Hadley

It felt like we'd walked to the ends of the Earth by the time we stopped to rest for more than five minutes. The sun had set. The moon had risen and sunk again. And the sun was high in the sky once again. Brecken had walked beside me the entire way. Until he stopped and gestured for me to get behind him as he hunkered down on the ground, deep in the foliage, knees bent while he dug through his pack. Not a single word was spoken as we drank from the canteen and each ate another protein bar. A quick peek inside his pack revealed his seemingly endless stash of them was almost entirely exhausted. Only two bars remained, and I was nervous about what this meant for our journey.

The idea of going hungry again after my experience with my captors scared me so much I almost couldn't swallow the bar I was eating, but I forced myself to choke it down and trust in Brecken. He hadn't steered me wrong yet, and I'd already displayed my faith by having sex with him under the waterfall. Thinking about how it felt to have him move inside me soothed my nerves, shifting my focus away from my fears while I relived one of the best moments of my life.

"Here's the plan." Brecken's voice, as soft as it was, startled me out of my thoughts and made me jerk. "My team should be here in the next thirty minutes or so. They'll arrive by chopper,"—he pointed towards an opening in front of us about fifty feet away—"landing right there."

The point where he'd pointed didn't seem big enough for a helicopter to land. "Are you sure it'll fit?"

Brecken flashed me a quick grin. "As certain as I was that I'd fit inside your tight pussy."

I slapped his arm, covering my mouth to stifle my laughter since I didn't think I could laugh as quietly as we were talking.

"Sorry, I couldn't resist."

He didn't sound the least bit sorry, but that was okay with me because his joke lightened the moment. "Uh-huh, sure you are. I'll remember that the first time you open the door for a *that's what she said* joke."

"I'm looking forward to it." The humor drained from his face, his expression turning serious again. "We need to stay hidden while we wait. I want you to rest, and I'll keep watch. The ground won't be very comfortable, but I can't hold you on my lap out here because I need to be ready for anything."

My head swiveled as my gaze darted around us. "Do you think we're in danger here?"

"We're a good distance away from the kidnappers, and I haven't seen any signs of them tracking us here. But that doesn't mean we're in the clear and the chopper is going to attract attention from anyone nearby."

"Okay, I'll be ready too," I whispered.

Brecken tilted my chin up with one long finger, staring me straight in the eyes. "I need you to rest, to gather your strength in case anything goes wrong when they get here. If this goes sideways, I need to know you'll be able to make a run for the chopper while I cover your back."

"No," I gasped, shaking my head. "I'm not going to make a run for safety and leave you behind."

This time his smile was blinding. "That's my precious girl." He dropped a kiss on my lips, pulling away to whisper against my mouth. "All the training in the world didn't prepare me for you. If you're in the line of fire, my concentration will be for shit. The best thing you can do for me is haul ass for the chopper and trust me to get us both out of here safely. Can you do that for me, Hadley?"

"Yes." It was the only acceptable answer because it was what he needed to hear from me. But if the opportunity came for me to do more? Well, that was something we could argue about later.

We settled in for the wait, me with my back to a tree and Brecken directly in front of me. He was alert, his head turning to scan our surroundings every few minutes and one of his guns at the ready. It gave me too much time to think. As we sat in silence, my nerves found something else to focus on—what was going to happen next. Brecken had been hired by my dad, but I wasn't sure I was ready to go back home. To face him and the role he played in what had happened to me. He'd let me rot in that hellhole for two weeks before sending Brecken in to save me. I was already pissed at him because of the whole arms dealing thing, and the situation took my anger to new heights. I didn't know how we were going to move past this.

Then there was Brecken. I'd given him my virginity, but no promises were exchanged between us. It would be crazy for me to think he wanted a real relationship with me. This might not be anything more than a heat of the moment thing for him. I wanted to pretend it was only that for me, but it wasn't. If it had been anyone other than Brecken who had rescued me, things would have gone differently. The circumstances behind us meeting might have lowered my inhibitions and made me act out of character, but only because the attraction was already there between us. I'd never felt the same pull towards another guy, and I didn't think I ever would. Our relationship started under intense circumstances, but I wanted it to last. There was no way for me to know if Brecken wanted the same thing unless I asked him.

I gathered up my courage and lifted an arm to grip his arm. "Brecken," I started, only for him to interrupt.

"Yeah, I hear it too."

Hear what too? It took me a moment to realize the faint sound in the distance was the helicopter.

Brecken got to his feet and offered me a hand to help me up. "Let's go. Stay behind me and stay quiet so I don't get us killed."

"Get us killed?" I repeated softly, moving quickly to keep up with him.

"We've got company coming in hot."

I looked around us, seeing nothing. "We do?"

Brecken tapped his ear with his free hand, the other holding his gun, aimed ahead of us. "I just heard from Sera, the chopper didn't go unnoticed."

"Crap," I muttered.

"There's a group of armed men coming from that direction." He pointed directly across the clearing from where we were approaching it. "Five of them. We don't know if they're the ones who took you, but at this point it doesn't really matter who they are because they sure as fuck aren't friendlies coming to welcome my team to their neck of the jungle."

"What can I do?"

"Stay behind me until I tell you to make a run for it. My team will lay down cover fire for us while I cover your back."

He didn't have time to say anything else because all hell broke loose. The helicopter hovered over the opening in the trees and several men spilled from the jungle, guns up and firing at it. The sound was deafening, louder than I expected.

"Ready?" Brecken asked.

"But they haven't landed yet!"

"They don't need to land to get us out of here," he answered as a ladder dropped from the side of the open helicopter door to the ground. "It's time for you to haul ass now that they've realized this is an extraction.

Sure enough, he was right. Two of the bad guys started shooting at us instead of the helicopter. Brecken pushed me forward and returned fire. "Go!" he yelled.

I went, running like my life depended on it. Because it did, and so did Brecken's. With my focus narrowed on the ladder, I sprinted full-out until I reached it, knowing Brecken wouldn't follow until I'd reached the safety of the helicopter. As soon as I got close enough, I leapt for the second rung and hauled myself up. I scurried up a couple notches, ignoring the safety harness in favor of speed. Then the ladder was being hauled up and I hung on for dear life, my eyes closed while I whispered a prayer.

"She's in!" one of Brecken's teammates yelled, and the ladder was immediately lowered back down.

One of the men shoved me deeper into the helicopter, and I watched over his shoulder as Brecken ran towards the ladder, firing his gun as he went.

"Shit! I don't have a clear shot and the guy in blue is going to have Boss in his sights any second now."

The helicopter turned, jolting me forward, right towards the door I'd been hauled through moments before. My gaze landed on a spot of blue on the ground. It was a man, with his gun raised and pointed right where Brecken would be running past unless someone took this guy out before he got there. I couldn't let that happen and acted on instincts deeply engraved.

Springing forward, I unsnapped the shoulder harness of the guy who'd shoved me out of the way, drawing his Beretta out of the holster. I undid the side mounted safety and dove towards the opening, landing on my stomach and bracing myself as Brecken's teammate gripped my legs to prevent me from falling out.

Taking aim, I fired, pulling the trigger over and over again until the clip was empty. Fifteen shots in all, but they were unnecessary because the first one had found its mark straight in the heart of the man who'd been trying to kill Brecken.

Frantic, I glanced down at the ladder and found him hanging ten feet away from the opening as he was being hauled up. As soon as he cleared the entrance, the helicopter lifted higher into the air and turned over the treetops of the jungle, out of danger. Brecken hauled me into his arms, squeezing me tight before pulling away to look at me, shouting above the noise so I could hear him. "How the hell did you make that shot?"

"I guess one good thing has come from having an arms dealer for my father," I yelled back. "At least he taught me how to be a crack shot."

CHAPTER 9

BRECKEN

Arms dealer? It was damn loud up here with the sound of the motor, but she was close enough to me that I'd heard her clear as a bell. My fascination with Hadley had apparently driven me to fuck up on the research end of this mission because I hadn't done much looking into her father. He'd come to me on a referral from a well-respected Army General for fuck's sake. I hadn't seen the need to focus on him when a man I'd served under had vouched for him. Then, I'd become immersed in what I could find out about Hadley's life. As soon as I'd tracked her down, I hadn't waited to charge in and rescue her, assuming her kidnapping was connected to human trafficking and time was quickly dwindling before they moved her to somewhere I'd never be able to find her.

I held my tongue, resisting the urge to question Hadley and leveling Sera and Whit with a glare to ensure neither of them asked her what she was talking about. With her father's connection to the General, odds were high there was more to the story. The kind of more that usually came with a top secret stamp on the file. None of us were in the military anymore, but being civilians didn't mean we were going to discuss what could possibly be classified information with Hadley. Especially not when it was possible the discussion could put her in more danger. Hadley's safety was my top priority.

Whit drew my attention by waving an ear piece under my nose. I checked mine and confirmed it was working before realizing he meant for me to give it to Hadley, knowing damn well I'd be pissed if he put it in for her. I turned it on and slid it into place in her ear.

"It's a good thing for you that she knows how to shoot, Boss," Whit said, making Hadley smile. "Sera wouldn't have gotten to him in time, and I'm the worst shot of the lot of us, her included."

"Which is why we need to teach you how to fly one of these suckers," Devon replied from the pilot's seat. "To free me up to shoot."

"Or he could spend more time at the shooting range with me," Sera added. "Practice makes perfect."

"I don't know about that," Whit drawled, looking at Hadley. "When's the last time you were at a range?"

"Seven months ago."

Those three little words held so much nostalgia. I needed to ask her about it later when we were alone.

"See!" Whit crowed. "She was damn near perfect without a hint of practice in almost forever. I was at the range last week and couldn't have made the same shot she did. My point has been made, practice doesn't always make perfect. Natural ability factors in and Boss's girl was born to hold a gun."

"Enough," I barked out, feeling Hadley's muscles tense. Whit, Devon, Sera and I had each killed during our time in the military. Some of us more than others, something Whit took for granted since the body count from his explosives was damn high. But Hadley was a civilian, an innocent twenty-two-year-old woman. Based on her trembling, I was certain her only previous experience with guns had been firing at paper targets. She'd proven herself to be incredibly strong with how well she'd held up over the last day and a half, but killing a man was another thing entirely. After her kidnapping, her time spent with her captors and her escape, this very well could be the straw that broke the camel's back for her.

"Don't be a dipshit," Sera hissed, gesturing at Hadley.

She tugged on Whit's arm to move them to the side of the aircraft opposite of us, giving Hadley and me a small degree of privacy. I yanked our comms units out of our ears and gripped them in a fist, settling us on our side until my back was against the wall of the chopper and Hadley was seated on my lap facing me. I lowered my head, my mouth settling above her ear to ensure she could hear me over the noise from the chopper's motor.

"It was him or me, precious, and I for one am damn grateful you took the shot that saved my life."

She pulled back, staring at me with tears filling her pretty green eyes before she leaned up to answer me. "Me, too. I think that's the hardest part, knowing I don't regret taking a life. Not even a little bit. I know if I hadn't done it then you'd be dead, and that's something I couldn't live with."

When she was done speaking, her head dropped onto my shoulder and sobs shook her body. I held her close, running my hands down her back trying to soothe her as she cried for the rest of the long flight to the airstrip where a private plane waited for us. The chopper had been borrowed from the army base in Honduras, thanks to the General. Once we made contact with him, someone would be sent to pick it up from the airstrip since it was a short drive from the base.

The plane belonged to my best friend. I'd helped to save Morgan's woman a while back and he was happy to return the favor when I'd called him to see if he could help with our transportation on this mission. I hadn't wanted to trigger any red flags with our arrival, and he'd arranged for the flight into Honduras under the guise of business purposes, listing Devon as the pilot, Whit as the co-pilot and Sera and me as the only passengers—only we hadn't flown in under our own names and had used Morgan and his wife's credentials. It was risky, but the General had pulled some strings with his military contacts to make it work.

He'd also arranged for a military log to show Sera as flying into the base yesterday. The plan was for her to fly back with us on her own passport while Hadley and I entered the United States as Morgan and Angelica, who would meet us at the private airport when we had our "emergency landing" and exchange places with us before the plane was "repaired" and continued on to the final destination where Customs would board the plane. The plan was risky because I wasn't sure if the fake passports I'd had made for Hadley and I would hold up if we weren't able to make the switch, but I didn't want anyone to know she was back in the States.

I also didn't want her captors to connect Hadley to me or my company. Not until I was able to pinpoint who'd been the one to order her kidnapping. Then they wouldn't need to link us together because they'd be too busy trying to stay alive to worry about Hadley. I'd collected a lot of contacts during my time in the military, made friends and saved lives. Many favors were owed to me, and I'd call in every single one if that's what it took to ensure her safety. A message needed to be sent— Hadley was off limits—and I was the man who'd make sure it was received loud and clear by anyone who thought to use her as a pawn in the future.

Even if it turned out that her father and the General were in bed with the bad guys somehow, Hadley was officially out of this mess. She wasn't her father's responsibility anymore. She was mine, and I'd do whatever was necessary to keep her safe and happy, right where she belonged. With me.

As I led her from the chopper and across the airstrip to the plane, it was as though she was in sync with me. She asked a question directly in line with what I was thinking, the perfect question for me to be able to keep her by my side.

"Where are we going? Is there anywhere in the world where I'll be safe?"

"Yes, Hadley. There's most definitely somewhere you can go to be safe. You're coming home with me." *And that's where you'll stay once this is all over, too.* At least I was smart enough to only think the last part and didn't blurt it out and scare her half to death.

CHAPTER 10

HADLEY

Brecken wanted me to go home with him. His words kept replaying in my head as we all transferred from the helicopter to the plane. Brecken and I took the seats in the back of the plane. Sera sat near the front, and Whit and Devon went into the cockpit. I gripped Brecken's hand during takeoff. After going through hell, my fear of flying seemed silly but it was still at the back of my mind. Then a miracle happened, something which had never been in the realm of possibility during any of my previous flights, the motion of the plane lulled me to sleep. I woke up to the sound of the landing gear going down and found myself with my head in Brecken's lap, his fingers running through my hair. The feeling was incredibly soothing, but I jerked up when the plane landed with a bump.

"We're safe and sound in the States now, Hadley," Brecken reassured me.

"But what about Customs?" I worried aloud. "I don't have any paperwork with me. Nothing to prove who I am, let alone that I'm an American citizen."

I heard the screech of brakes and then Sera jumped up from her seat and got to work at opening the plane door.

"No need," Brecken answered, undoing my seat belt and tugging me behind him as he strode down the aisle between the seats. By the time we made it to the door, the stairs were down and a hot guy with a beautiful younger woman was climbing up them. "We're getting off here."

"It's good to see you made it back without damaging my plane," the guy joked, slapping Brecken on the back as he moved past us.

"Oh, stop it, Morgan," the girl scolded, flashing me a quick grin. "We both know you couldn't care less about the plane. Even if you did, it wouldn't matter since you owe him a debt which can never be repaid."

I wondered what Brecken could have done for this man to be in his debt to such an extent that the loss of a private plane would be negligible. Morgan pulled the woman into his lap as he sat down in the aisle seat in the front row. The love in his gaze as he looked at her was evident to anyone seeing them together. "You're right, Angel. Without him, I wouldn't have been able to save you and all the planes in the world wouldn't come close to the loss that would have been."

Mystery solved then. Brecken had helped save her life, just as he'd done with me. If I was lucky, maybe he'd come to look at me the way Morgan gazed at his Angel.

"No time to chat," Sera growled at us. "You need to get out of here before air traffic control realizes we stopped. This might be a tiny airport, but we can't count on them being completely oblivious."

"You heard the woman," Morgan replied. "I left the engine running. I bought the car yesterday and the title work is in your name. There's a cooler in the back that Angel packed for you, and you'll find a suitcase filled with clothes, toiletries and the papers you had overnighted to me."

"It sounds like you thought of everything," Brecken called out as we made our way down the stairs.

"You didn't even say thank you," I pointed out when he climbed into the driver's seat after getting me belted in on the passenger's side.

"We don't usually do the thank you thing," he replied. "Morgan's my best friend."

"Wow," I breathed. "Your best friend does stuff like loaning you his plane and buying you a car?"

"Not usually, but this mission was different."

"Different?" I repeated. Could what I was thinking be true? Had he been serious when he'd said I'd been precious to him from the moment he saw my photo? Had he really reached out to his friend because of what he felt for me from the start? "Because of me?"

He reached across the console to squeeze my hand. "Haven't you figured it out yet, Hadley? I'd do just about anything for you."

I cocked my head and studied him as he raced out of the service entrance to the private airport and headed for the highway. As hard as it was to believe since we'd only met two days ago, I had faith he was telling me the truth. Although the sun was setting in the sky, I could still see his face clearly. His eyes were focused on the road ahead of us, but his expression was determined, as though keeping me safe was his most important mission. My heart raced in my chest as butterflies took flight in my stomach.

"I feel the same way about you, Brecken."

His hand tightened around mine and he briefly glanced my way, male satisfaction in his gaze. "You already did all you need to do, my precious girl. It's my job to take care of you from here on out."

With his declaration, my heart melted and I was filled with the resolve to make sure this relationship, whatever it was, didn't end up being one-sided. I wanted to give to Brecken at least as much as I took from him. It was the one thought which kept replaying in my head as we raced through the evening, heading towards Brecken's home. "I don't even know where you live," I mumbled.

Brecken must have had exceptional hearing because he caught what I said. "Chicago."

"Is that where we're headed?"

"It is," he confirmed.

It was dark outside and there wasn't much traffic on the road with us. "Any idea when we'll need to stop?"

"I'd like to go until we need to stop for gas in about an hour or so, if that works for you."

I turned my head away from him to hide my sly grin. "It's more than okay with me."

Taking a deep breath, I gave myself a silent pep talk. Life was short. I was stronger than I knew. I could do anything if I set my mind to it. Even this.

I unlaced my fingers from his grip and lifted his arm to place it over my shoulder. Then I undid my seat belt and leaned sideways in my seat to whisper in his ear. "Remember back at the waterfall when I said I wanted to taste you too?"

His arm dropped down, his hand tightening on the back of my neck and holding me in place. "Yes," he hissed out. "But you don't need to do it like this."

I pushed against his hold to look into his eyes. "What if I want to do it exactly like this? To have my first blow job happen with you right here in the front seat while you're driving me to the safety of your home?"

"Fuck, Hadley," he groaned, his hand clenching. "How the hell am I supposed to say no to something like that?"

"You're not," I breathed out. "You should give in and let me do exactly what I want."

He released my neck, moving his hand down my back. With his other hand, he set the cruise control right at the speed limit and undid his cargo pants, unzipping the fly and shoving his boxers down. His dick jutted out, fully hard. It was all the permission I needed. I reached down and gave it a few tentative strokes.

"Feels so damn good."

The huskiness of Brecken's voice made me bold, or bolder than I was already being. I strengthened my grip on him and rose to my knees in my seat. Bending forward, I moved my hand from his dick to the side of his seat and placed the other on the handbrake for leverage. Once I was positioned the right way, I dipped my head and licked the tip of his dick, enjoying the salty taste of the drop of pre-come I gathered on my tongue. His answering groan told me how much he was enjoying my actions and spurred me on more.

Sliding my mouth halfway down his length, I suck at him eagerly. My cheek muscles were straining to fit him into my mouth and I struggled to take more of his dick.

"Work your mouth up and down on me."

I began to slide my mouth up and down his shaft, moaning when I felt the muscles of his leg tighten under me and his fist clench in the fabric of my shirt. I moaned against his flesh at the feeling of power that coursed through my veins.

"Fuck," he hissed. "Do that again."

I moaned again, letting him feel the vibrations from my throat. His hand moved up, tangling in my hair as he began to guide the movements of my head.

"Can you suck me harder?"

"Mmmm-hmmm." It was the only answer I could manage while my mouth was full of his dick. That and the pumping of my cheek muscles against his shaft while I opened and closed my lips around his length. It was more than enough, though. His hips jerked up and there was a loud gasp above me.

"You better pull away unless you want me to come in your mouth."

I didn't pull away. Instead, I sucked harder until I felt the jet of his come hit the back of my throat. I held still as his dick twitched in my mouth, swallowing when I finally lifted my head. Licking my lips, I sat up and shifted back into my seat, blushing.

"Marry me." I felt the blood drain from my face, removing all traces of my embarrassment at my boldness.

"What?" I gasped, certain I hadn't heard him right.

He pulled over to the side of the road, put the car in park and turned to face me. Pulling my hands into his own, he looked deeply into my eyes. "Marry me," he repeated.

"I guess I must be really good at blow jobs," I joked.

"You are," he agreed, his lip tilting up in a grin. "But that's not why I'm asking. The last name change may help me to hide you."

My heart dropped. This was definitely the least romantic proposal in the history of the world. I crossed my arms over my chest, a protective shield I suddenly felt I needed for this conversation. "Don't you think marriage is a little excessive?"

Brecken reached down and rested his hand on my belly. "You're going to become my wife one way or another."

"How romantic," I sighed, rolling my eyes.

"And you could be pregnant with my baby already."

Chapter 11

Brecken

"Holy crap," she breathed out, her already pale complexion turning another shade lighter. Her hand moved over mine, holding it in place while she stared at me in amazement. "I might be pregnant."

"That's what happens when you have sex without a condom."

"We had sex without a condom."

She sounded like a parrot repeating after me, and it was fucking adorable. "We did."

It was much less adorable when she punched my arm—until she shook her fist out while practically hopping in her seat. "Crap, crap, crap," she chanted. "You're built like a brick wall."

I pulled her hand towards my lips and kissed it gently. "And you're avoiding the question."

My precious girl demonstrated her bravery once again by taking a deep breath and blurting out her concern. "If I'm not pregnant, would you still want me to be your wife? Because if so, I think we should wait, even if it means it will be easier for the bad guys to track me down. I might not approve of how my dad earns his money, but even though I haven't talked to my parents in six months, I still want a marriage like theirs. I want my husband and me to be a team."

"I want the same thing." I knew I was fucking this up, not explaining it to Hadley well. Even worse, I was making her think I wasn't serious about my proposal. Digging deep, I tried to find the words to convince her to say yes. "For you to be my teammate, I mean. I didn't have the best example of marriage with my parents, but one thing the military taught me was the importance of knowing you can rely on your team. I know it's insane for me to know this already, hell I gave Morgan a hard time for moving Angelica into his house the day he met her and here I am trying to convince you to marry me two days after you met me."

My chuckle held no humor because I had too much riding on this to find it funny. I saw something working behind her pretty green eyes as I spoke, so I pushed forward and hoped for the best. "Baby or no baby, I want you to be my wife. I should never have presented this to you as a way to better protect you. That was me being an ass and using the situation to my advantage to try to avoid admitting to the real reason I'm asking you. And that reason is I want my ring on your finger, my last name after your first and you living in my home. Not just for the short term, either. I want it forever."

Tears were streaming down her face in earnest, and they worried the fuck out of me. I hoped like hell they weren't a sign of me fucking this up even more. When a huge grin split her face, my lungs seized. And then she gave me the answer I'd been waiting for.

"Yes, I'll marry you."

Wrapping my hands under her armpits, I lifted her over the console and onto my lap. I captured her lips with mine and sealed our promises to each other with a kiss. When I finally lifted my head, her cheeks were dry and her eyes were dazed.

"Tomorrow."

She smiled up at me. "Tomorrow what?"

"I want you to marry me tomorrow in Kentucky."

"What about blood tests, waiting periods and a marriage license?"

I held up my hand and ticked off each point with a finger. "Kentucky doesn't require a blood test, has no waiting period and we can get a marriage license in the morning by applying at a County Clerk's office."

She looked to the side for a moment, her eyebrows raised in surprise, before meeting my gaze again. "You sound awfully familiar with how weddings work in Kentucky."

"I might have looked it up when I was planning our route home," I mumbled, and this time it was me who looked away.

Her laughter rang out loudly in the car and I couldn't stop myself from bringing my gaze right back to her. "You should have started your proposal with that information. It would have gone a long way towards convincing me you were serious if you'd planned this out before we had sex," she teased. "Unless this is a plan you use for all the women you save."

Her voice sounded like she was still joking, but the look in her eyes worried me. "This is the first time I've ever planned, or even thought about, my marriage to anyone. It's you. Only you."

The breath she must have been holding whooshed out. "Good," she murmured.

"That's good, but what about identification? I didn't think to bring any with me for my kidnapping."

Turning in my seat, I dug through the front, zippered pocket in the suitcase Morgan had packed for me and found the envelope I'd had Hadley's parents send to his home. I opened it and pulled out her driver's license, birth certificate and social security card.

"Those are mine!" she gasped, grabbing them from my hand. "How did you get them?"

"I called your parents and told them I might need them as part of your rescue."

She rolled her eyes at me. "Aren't you the guy who had a fake passport made for me without me even having my photo taken for it?"

"Yes, but this needs to be real. I refuse to leave any doubt as to the legality of our marriage."

"It sounds like you thought of everything except for what I'll wear and who will marry us."

I pulled my phone from my pocket, checked my text messages and found a reply to the message I'd sent right before we landed to an Army buddy who lived in Kentucky. "A friend of mine knows a retired judge who will be happy to officiate our marriage." I jerked my thumb towards the bag in the back seat. "And I'm pretty sure you'll find a couple dresses in there for you."

Her gaze darted to the bag and then she moved her seat back all the way down to lean across it and open the suitcase, then pulled out three dresses, two were white and one was cream. "I can't believe you managed all of this in the middle of rescuing me from kidnappers in the Nicaraguan jungle. You don't happen to have a secret superhero identity, do you?"

"That depends." I waggled my eyebrows at her and lifted a piece of white lingerie out of the suitcase. "If I did, would it improve my odds of seeing you in this?"

Her eyes widened in surprise. "I've never worn anything like it before." A growl rumbled up my throat, making her giggle. "But I'm pretty sure you could talk me into it since I've done a lot of things with you that are new to me."

"I want you to do all those things with me." Especially the ones involving lingerie went without saying.

"Then let's go cross the biggest one off the list and get hitched."

How quickly she forgot I might have already knocked her up. It was cute how she thought it was the biggest one, but to me becoming parents was at the top of the list. I couldn't wait to see her belly round with my child. If she wasn't pregnant already, I'd have to do my best to correct that once we made it to the safety of my penthouse condo.

I was a man of action, always had been and it had served me well in the past. Things were bad at home when I was eighteen, so I enlisted to find a way out. I'd flourished in the Army, finding my niche and serving my country. When I decided a total separation after ten years was the right plan for me, I held firm during my talks with my career counselor, my supervisor and my OIC. It didn't matter how often they told me another ten years would buy me a retirement—I had a feeling I wouldn't make it and would be dead by then. Without a college degree and with a unique set of skills I'd picked up during my time in the military, I knew I needed a plan for success. I reached out to Morgan, and with his help my security business was born. The rest was history, as they say.

Each of those decisions led me to this point, as I stood beside the most gorgeous woman in the world and faced the retired judge who would marry us. My buddy arranged for a couple of witnesses, too. All we'd needed to do was grab a license and show up. I'd made a quick detour to a florist's shop when I'd noticed Hadley looking at it with longing out the window of the car as we drove past. I was rushing her into this marriage, possibly taking advantage of her when she was vulnerable from the kidnapping and killing a man to keep me safe, but I wanted this ceremony to be as perfect as possible for her because this was the only time she'd get married. It was one and done for her. Once she was legally mine, I wasn't letting her go.

I listened avidly as she repeated after the judge, promising to share her life with me from today forward. Then it was my turn, and my voice rang clear and true as I spoke the words which were truer than any others I'd ever said.

"I, Brecken Kane, take you, Hadley Gresham, to be my wife. I will share my life with you, building our dreams together, supporting you through times of trouble, and rejoicing with you in times of happiness. I promise to give you all of my respect, love and loyalty through the trials and triumphs of our lives together. This commitment is made in love, kept in faith, and made new every day of our lives."

By the time I was done, tears streamed down her cheeks. She'd managed to make it through her vows without crying, but hearing mine made her weep.

"Are you exchanging rings?" the judge asked.

Hadley's fingers trembled in my grasp as she shook her head, her cheeks pinkening. I released one of them to dig in the pocket of the suit pants Morgan had packed for me and retrieved a small black box. Thumbing it open, my gaze darted up to Hadley's face when she gasped. Her eyes were locked on the ring, a flawless diamond solitaire set in platinum. It was bigger than I'd expected, but that wasn't a surprise since Morgan had picked it up for me. My best friend wasn't exactly known for being subtle, something for which I was deeply grateful when I spotted the look of wonder on my precious girl's face.

"That's definitely a ring." The judge's tone was dry, drawing a giggle from Hadley.

"It looks like my fiancé really did think of everything."

I stole a quick kiss from her lips before sliding two of the rings from the box, holding them at the tip of her finger and waiting for the judge to continue.

"Your wedding ring is the visible sign of the invisible bond which unites your two hearts in love."

"A visible sign nobody will be able to miss," Hadley whispered.

The judge coughed to cover a chuckle at her aside. "Brecken, please place the ring on Hadley's finger and repeat after me."

I followed his instruction without glancing down, staring into Hadley's eyes instead. I wanted her to see how much this moment meant to me.

"Hadley, I give you this ring. Wear it with love and joy. As this ring has no end, my love for you is also forever."

"Is there a ring in there for you too, Brecken?"

Hadley cocked a brow at me in question before glancing down and catching sight of the matching men's wedding band. "Yes, there is," she answered, lifting it off the velvet interior.

"Hadley, place the ring on Brecken's finger and repeat after me."

Her voice didn't tremble as she slid the ring on me. "With this ring, I marry you. Wear this ring forever as a sign of my love."

"May the wedding rings you exchanged today remind you always that you are surrounded by deep and abiding love."

I knew what was next and didn't wait, claiming my wife's lips in a passionate kiss that had her gasping for air once I was done. She was officially mine, and I had the papers to prove it.

CHAPTER 12

HADLEY

The six-hour drive from the little town south of Lexington to Brecken's home in Chicago flew past as we talked about all the things most couples would discuss during the first week or two of dating. Our childhoods, favorite books and movies, all the little things that made us who we were. We were doing it backwards since we were already married, but it didn't matter because we'd learned the truly important stuff about each other back in the Nicaraguan jungle. Not only had we made it through hell together, but we'd spent more hours in each other's company than most couples would after a couple months of dating.

The parking garage he pulled into was dark and kind of scary. I was a little uncertain until the elevator, which required a passcode to use, took us straight to the penthouse and the doors opened to the foyer of a gorgeous apartment. I started to walk out, but

Brecken surprised me by sweeping me into his arms.

"I believe it's customary for the groom to carry the bride over the threshold." His voice was a whisper of sound, his breath hot against my ear as he carried me into the living room before setting me on my feet.

The design was all black leather and shiny chrome, a bachelor pad fit to grace the pages of a home décor magazine. There was a giant flat screen television on one wall and what looked like a gourmet kitchen across the open space. But the most impressive part of the apartment was the floor to ceiling windows overlooking Lake Michigan. I was drawn to them as though by an invisible string, placing my palms against the cold glass as I looked outside at the incredible view.

I didn't hear Brecken approach me from behind, but I felt him when he pressed me against the window. The contrast between the heat of his body and the glass, chilled from the outside temperature, sent a shiver through me. The view blurred as Brecken twisted me in his arms until I was facing him. Then his lips crashed down on mine, our tongues tangling together while his hands made quick work of the removal of our clothes, leaving him completely naked and me standing in nothing but my tiny, white lace panties.

When he tore his mouth from mine and wrapped his lips around one of my nipples, I moaned and tangled my hands in his hair to hold his head in place. Mewling and rubbing against him, I was close to the edge just from the attention he lavished on my breasts—licking, sucking and nibbling at the sensitive flesh. My back arched and my hips moved restlessly against him in search of more contact. A silent request he answered by dipping his fingers into my panties, sliding them through my wetness. His mouth lifted from my nipple, and I watched as he replaced it with his drenched fingers.

"I could live on the taste of your pussy alone," he growled. "But as much as I want to eat at you for hours, it's going to have to wait because I need to be inside you. Now."

"I need you just as much."

His eyes darkened further at my response. He claimed my mouth one more time, letting me taste myself on his lips before he spun me around to face the window again. I raised my hands and placed them on the glass to brace myself, widening my stance and tilting my hips to give him better access. His hands slid around my hips, thumbs resting on the small of my back. He leaned over and whispered in my ear. "So fucking beautiful, seeing you spread out for me like this."

Then the heat of his body was gone except for the feel of his legs outside mine as he lined his dick up with my entrance and drove into me with one powerful thrust. There was none of the pain from our last time, only the intense pleasure of his hardened length sliding against my inner walls. "So good," I moaned.

"And so fucking tight." His fingers dug into my hips as he pulled out and plunged back in, over and over again. He went deeper and faster with each ram of his hips. "My wife."

His voice held a purring satisfaction at being able to call me his. It made my pussy flutter against him. "My husband," I gasped, sending him into a frenzy.

"Your pussy is mine, my precious girl," he growled into my ear, pushing me against the glass as he hammered into me. His hand slid up my back, along my arm and down to my hand. "This ring marks you as mine for all the world to see, but I want to leave other brands on your body. Ones for my eyes only."

I felt the scrape of his stubble before his teeth sunk into my shoulder. The sharp sting made me shudder with pleasure. When he didn't let go, holding me submissive underneath him, the way a lion would his lioness, while he thrust in and out, I exploded. "Brecken!" I screamed.

With my pussy clenching around him, Brecken followed me with a shout, his hot come pouring into me. When my heartbeat calmed enough for me to catch my breath, I giggled. "Bedded, wedded and bedded again. All in three days' time, too."

His chest shook against my back as he laughed. We stood like that for a few minutes, laughing together with him deep inside me, before he pulled out and lifted me into his arms. "I think I can do better once I get you in our bed."

Ours, I liked the sound of that. He carried me down a hallway and into the bedroom, gently placing me on the mattress before landing on top of me. Then he proceeded to show me how much better he could do, several times through the night.

I rolled over, enjoying the feel of the cool sheets against my naked skin and reached out for Brecken. Finding his side of the bed empty, I sat up in surprise. Brecken hadn't left me alone without waking me up for a morning quickie in the week since we'd arrived in Chicago. I wandered into the connecting master bath and noticed the mirror was still fogged as I washed my hands and brushed my teeth. I couldn't be too far behind him. Maybe he'd planned to surprise me with breakfast in bed. Moving towards the door, I halted in my tracks with my hand on the knob when I heard voices coming from the living room.

"So much for the idea of breakfast in bed," I muttered to myself as I entered the walk-in closet and put on a pair of silk pajamas, throwing a robe over it before I headed down the hallway. Finding my parents seated on our couch across from Brecken was quite the shock. My small gasp of surprise alerted them to my presence, and all eyes turned to me. My husband rose from his seat and moved towards me swiftly, but my gaze remained locked on my parents. I hadn't seen them in more than half a year. And we hadn't spoken, not once during all that time.

I didn't understand what was happening. Brecken knew how much our estrangement pained me, but he also knew the reason for it. I thought he understood how I felt about what my dad did for a living. When we'd made the drive to Chicago last week, I'd been surprised by Brecken's story about how he'd met my father. I couldn't fathom a reason for the connection between my dad, the illegal arms dealer, and a well-respected General in the Army. He'd asked me a lot of questions about my parents, but I figured it was all part of the getting to know you process. Apparently I thought wrong and his questions were for another purpose.

"Morning, precious." He dropped a kiss on my lips as though this morning was the same as any other. Then he moved his head until his mouth rested above my ear. "I know you're scared, but I need you to trust me here. I did some checking into your dad's company over the last week. Some things didn't add up so I dug further. What I found will surprise you, Hadley. In a good way, but your dad asked if he could be the one to explain it to you. That's why they're here."

My heart filled with hope as I gripped Brecken's hand and turned to face my parents. My mom's eyes were full of happy tears when we sat down across from them, Brecken settling me on his lap with his arms wrapped around me.

"You look so happy," she whispered.

"I am," I confirmed in a soft voice, sending her a quick smile before shifting my gaze to my dad. My voice hardened when I continued. "Now. But I was the furthest thing from happy when Brecken found me in the jungle after your associates took me from my dorm room and you left me there to rot for two weeks, wondering if you were just going to let me die because I hadn't forgiven you yet."

"Hadley, no!" My dad jumped to his feet, pacing back and forth behind the couch where he'd been sitting, one hand running through his hair. "You're my daughter, and I love you. I *never* wanted anything to happen to you, that's why I pushed you away in the first place."

I jerked in Brecken's arms. "What the heck do you mean, pushed me away?"

He moved around the couch, and I froze in place until he dropped down beside my mom. "I arranged for you to discover my illegal arms dealings." He made air quotes when he said the last three words. "Which aren't so much as illegal as they are sanctioned by the US government."

"You lied to me?" I gasped.

He stared straight at me, anguish evident in his eyes. "I did, but it was necessary. I was working on a project." He cleared his throat and shifted his gaze to Brecken for a moment before looking at me again. "I can't go into a lot of details because they're classified, but Brecken can confirm that everything I'm telling you is the honest to God truth."

"I can, precious," my husband whispered in my ear.

I nodded and my dad continued with his explanation. "My situation put me in a unique position to help the Army in their search for an enemy who'd managed to get their hands on a weapon they needed to get back. Badly."

"Badly is an understatement," Brecken added. "Your dad didn't have much of a choice. Too many lives were at stake."

My dad waved it away, like him helping to save lives didn't matter. "It was a decision I quickly came to regret because the only way to insert myself with them was to take possession of something else they wanted and to play coy in an effort to draw them out. Only it backfired, and threats were made against my family. Against you specifically, presumably because you were the easiest to access since your mom spends most of her time behind the gates of our home."

"Your solution was to push me away? Wouldn't that have put me at risk even more?"

"The profiler involved with the case assured me that their leader would lose interest in you if it appeared that I couldn't care less." His head hung low, and his voice dropped. "So we spread a story about you not being my biological daughter and I told them we weren't even speaking to each other and that I'd finally been successful at removing you completely from your mother's life."

My mom took his hand in hers. "He would have pushed me away too if they'd been able to figure out a story that made sense."

"The men the Army was hunting are beyond dangerous. They're vicious and bloodthirsty, and I was willing to do whatever it took to keep you safe. Even if it meant you hated me forever. But they somehow figured out our ruse and took you. I just about went crazy trying to get the Army to help me search for you. To help me rescue you," he pleaded. "Eventually, the General put me in touch with a man who he said was your best bet."

"Brecken," I sighed.

"The General was right. He managed to get you out."

"The guys who took me, are they still out there?"

A look passed between the two men, I wasn't certain what it meant but it seemed to hold a promise. "Not for long," my dad answered.

My situation had been desperate when Brecken had rescued me in the jungle. Before that, I'd spent so many months thinking my dad was a horrible person, responsible for the deaths of others. Brecken had managed to restore my faith in him. I had a feeling I was going to spend the rest of my life with him accomplishing impossible feats to make sure I was happy.

"I never thought in a million years that I'd be thankful for being taken the way I was, but I am because it brought me to Brecken."

My husband's arms tightened around me as my parent's gazes dropped to the hand I extended, showing off the rings Brecken had placed there. I meant every word, too. I'd endure it all over again if he was waiting for me at the end. Our relationship had been forged in the fires of hell. It would withstand the test of time.

Epilogue

Brecken

"It's done," the voice in my ear delivered the news I'd waited almost a month to hear. The man who'd ordered Hadley's kidnapping was dead, along with all of his men who'd been involved in taking her and holding her captive.

"Did you get out clean?"

"Do you even have to ask?" he growled.

"Sorry," I sighed, knowing damn well he wouldn't leave a trace behind. He was the best of the best, trained by the Army, and he owed me a favor. One that was now paid in full and then some. "I'm in your debt."

"And don't think I'll forget it." He hung up right as Hadley raced into my home office and leapt into my lap, twining her arms around my neck.

"Guess what?" she asked, bouncing up and down with excitement. "I took my last test online and am officially done with college!"

"I'm damn proud of you, precious." The General had pulled some strings and had the FBI approach the president of her school about her kidnapping. They didn't provide any details and informed him that the matter was being kept under wraps for her safety. The school was appalled to learn she'd been taken from her dorm and was more than happy to keep it quiet. They were willing to agree to almost anything to make that happen, including making special arrangements so she could catch up on her missed work and finish off all her classes online. She'd missed graduation, but she'd earned her degree all the same.

"There was another test I took this morning, too." Her tone softened, and I watched in amazement as she wiggled in my lap and pulled a little white stick out of her pocket. She flipped it over and showed me the results window where two pink lines were visible.

"Two lines means pregnant, right?"

She nodded, beaming at me. "It does."

I buried my face in her shoulder. "I fucking love you," I mumbled against her skin.

"You better," she giggled. "Because it's too late to get rid of me now that you've put your baby in my belly."

"I've told you before and I'll tell you again—you've been mine since the moment I saw your photo. There will be no getting rid of anyone in this marriage."

"How about you show me instead?"

I dropped one hand down to cup her pussy. "That would be my pleasure."

"And mine," she moaned as I slid my hand down the front of her yoga pants and slid a finger inside her pussy.

"Definitely yours too," I promised.

I did a thorough job of seeing to her pleasure, taking my time until she was begging me to let her come. "Please, please, please," she chanted.

I pulled my fingers out of her pussy, making her mewl in protest until I shoved her pants down and unzipped my own to pull my cock out. I nudged her pussy with the tip and she whimpered with need.

"Now," she pleaded. I thrust up into her, fucking her until I had wrung several orgasms from her and let myself come. Her head dropped on my shoulder, and her body melted into mine. Enjoying the feel of her in my arms, I couldn't help but think that today couldn't get any better. The men who had been a danger to her were dead. She was pregnant with my baby. And I'd fucked her to sleep on my lap with me still inside her. After all the darkness, a bright future lay ahead of me—and I owed it all to the sleeping beauty in my arms.

OTHER BOOKS BY THIS AUTHOR

BLYTHE COLLEGE SERIES

Push the Envelope

Hit the Wall

Summer Nights (novella duo)

Outside the Box

Winter Wedding (novella)

BACHELORETTE PARTY SERIES

Sucked Into Love

CRISIS SERIES

Identity Crisis

BLACK RIVER PACK SERIES

Crying Wolf

Shoot for the Moon

Thrown to the Wolves

McMAHON CLAN SERIES

Bear the Consequences

Bear It All

Bear the Burden

BODY & SOUL SERIES

Bare Your Soul

About the Author

I absolutely adore reading—always have and always will. When I was growing up, my friends used to tease me when I would trail after them, trying to read and walk at the same time. If I have downtime, odds are you will find me reading or writing.

I am the mother of two wonderful sons who have inspired me to chase my dream of being an author. I want them to learn from me that you can live your dream as long as you are willing to work for it.

When I told my mom that my new year's resolution was to self-publish a book in 2013, she pretty much told me, "About time!"

Connect with me online!

Facebook:

http://www.facebook.com/rochellepaigeauthor

Twitter:

@rochellepaige1

Goodreads:

https://www.goodreads.com/author/show/7328358.Rochelle_Paige

Website:

http://www.rochellepaige.com

55677594R00067

Made in the USA
Charleston, SC
04 May 2016